Just Like You

By Sarah Albee • Illustrated by Tom Brannon

A Random House PICTUREBACK® Book

Random House 🏠 New York

Copyright © 2002 Sesame Workshop. Sesame Street Muppets copyright © 2002 Sesame Workshop.
All rights reserved under International and Pan-American Copyright Conventions.
Published in the United States of America by Random House, Inc., New York, and simultaneously in
Canada by Random House of Canada Limited, Toronto, in conjunction with Sesame Workshop. Sesame Street,
Sesame Workshop, and their logos are trademarks and service marks of Sesame Workshop.
Library of Congress Control Number: 2001088311   ISBN: 0-375-81588-0

Printed in the United States of America June 2002 10 9 8 7 6 5 4 3 2 1
www.randomhouse.com/kids/sesame   www.sesamestreet.com
PICTUREBACK, RANDOM HOUSE, and the Random House colophon are registered trademarks
and the Please Read to Me colophon is a trademark of Random House, Inc.

"We have a new student in our class, everyone," said Judy, Elmo's preschool teacher, one morning. "I'd like you all to meet Lizzie."

"Hi!" said Lizzie, waving her hand a little.

Elmo knew that it was not polite to stare. But he couldn't help it. He was looking at the chair that Lizzie was sitting in. It had wheels.

"Elmo, please show Lizzie where we put our lunch," said Judy.

Elmo put down his paintbrush. "You can put your lunch over here," he told Lizzie.

"Okay," said Lizzie. She used her hands to roll her chair toward the shelf.

"Why do you roll around in that chair?" asked Elmo.

"I can't walk," Lizzie explained. "I was born with something wrong with my legs. So I use this wheelchair to get around. I'm getting really good at it. My arms are strong."

She made a muscle, and Elmo touched it. "Wow!" he said. "You sure *are* strong!"

During art, Judy asked everyone to draw three of their favorite things. Elmo drew a green ice cream cone, a basketball, and a black-and-white puppy.

He was just finishing his drawing when Judy flicked the lights off and then on again.

"Circle time!" called Judy. She and the assistant teacher, Amber, had arranged the chairs in a circle.

"Let's start by showing the class our favorite-things drawings," Judy said when everyone was seated. "Lizzie? Why don't you go first?"

Lizzie held up her drawing. She had drawn a dog, an ice cream cone, and a basketball.

Elmo was surprised. "She likes the same things Elmo does!" he said to himself.

At snack time, Elmo hurried to sit next to Lizzie. "So, you like ice cream?" he asked her.

"Yeah!" said Lizzie. "My favorite is strawberry!"

"Elmo's favorite is pistachio, but strawberry is good, too. Do you like vegetables?" Elmo asked.

"Some," said Lizzie. "But not Brussels sprouts. I hate Brussels sprouts."

"So does Elmo!" agreed Elmo.

"Elmo," said Judy. "Why don't you show Lizzie around the school after snack time?"

"Do you want Elmo to push you?" Elmo asked Lizzie as they left the classroom for their tour.

"No thanks, I can do it myself," said Lizzie. "I go to physical therapy. That's where I learn how to make my body stronger. I'm learning how to hop over little bumps with my front wheels."

"Gee, you *are* good at that," said Elmo. "Here are the drinking fountains. There's a high one and a low one."

"The lower one is meant for people in wheelchairs, so they can reach," Lizzie pointed out. "It's perfect for me."

"It's perfect for Elmo, too," Elmo said. "It's easier for Elmo to reach."

"The gym is upstairs," said Elmo, pointing. He looked at the wheels on Lizzie's chair. "Um, do you ever use the gym?"

"Sure I do!" said Lizzie. "See that ramp? That lets people in wheelchairs get up and down instead of using stairs. Besides, gym is my favorite part of the day!"

"Really?" said Elmo. "Same with Elmo!"

GYMNASIUM

Elmo showed Lizzie the bathroom.

"See that bar?" Lizzie pointed to a bar on the wall. "That's for people in wheelchairs to hold on to while they stand up and sit down. And that low sink makes it easy for me to wash my hands."

When Elmo and Lizzie got back to the classroom, everyone was getting ready to go outside to play. Amber came over to help Lizzie get her coat on.

"I'm still learning how to put on my own coat," said Lizzie. "That's one thing my physical therapist is helping me learn to do."

"Elmo's still kind of learning, too," said Elmo, struggling with his zipper.

"Here, Elmo, I already know how to zip," said Lizzie. She helped him zip up his coat.

Outside, the kids all helped build a snowman.

After recess, everyone was ready for a rest. Amber helped Lizzie out of her chair and onto a cot. Lizzie and Grover had the exact same blanket.

After rest time, Judy asked everyone to line up to go to the gym.

As they got near the gym, Big Bird stared down at Lizzie. "Are you coming to gym, too, Lizzie?" he asked her.

"Of course she is!" said Elmo. "It's her favorite part of the day!"

Amber helped push Lizzie up the ramp.

"Going up ramps is hard work all by myself," said Lizzie. "I need to save my energy for exercise!"

In gym, everyone chose a partner to play catch with. Elmo asked Lizzie to be his partner.

"Wow!" said Elmo. "Elmo wishes he could catch as well as you can!"

"Me too!" said Big Bird as his ball bounced off his toe.

"I'm learning how to dribble, too. I want to play on a wheelchair basketball team when I grow up," said Lizzie. "Or maybe be a basketball coach!"

"Are you coming back tomorrow, Lizzie?" asked Elmo at the end of the day.

"Yup," said Lizzie. "I'm in this class from now on."

"Your dad is here, Lizzie," said Judy. "And look who he brought with him!"

"My puppy!" squealed Lizzie. "Hey, Elmo, this is Cooper!"

"Gee," said Elmo. "He looks just like the picture you drew!"

"He's a she!" Lizzie told Elmo with a giggle. "Maybe you can come to my house and we can walk her together."

"And this is my dad," said Lizzie. "Dad, this is my new friend, Elmo."

"Hi!" said Elmo. "Lizzie is going to teach Elmo how to zip his jacket! And we're going to walk Cooper together."

Lizzie's dad smiled. "I'm sure Lizzie would love that, Elmo," he said.

"Bye, Elmo," said Lizzie. She held Cooper's paw up so that Cooper could wave good-bye, too.

"Elmo will see you soon, Cooper!" said Elmo. "And Elmo will see *you* tomorrow, Lizzie!"